Pup and Hound
Hatch an Egg

For Tannin and Tyler, egg hatchers
eggs-traordinaire! — S.H.

For those who might eggs-pect me to
dedicate a book to them — L.H.

Kids Can Read   Kids Can Read is a registered trademark of Kids Can Press Ltd
®

Text © 2007 Susan Hood
Illustrations © 2007 Linda Hendry

Kids Can Press acknowledges the financial support of the Government
of Ontario, through the Ontario Media Development Corporation's
Ontario Book Initiative; the Ontario Arts Council; the Canada Council
for the Arts; and the Government of Canada, through the BPIDP, for
our publishing activity.

Published in Canada by   Published in the U.S. by
Kids Can Press Ltd.   Kids Can Press Ltd.
29 Birch Avenue   2250 Military Road
Toronto, ON M4V 1E2   Tonawanda, NY 14150

www.kidscanpress.com

The artwork in this book was rendered in pencil crayons on sienna
colored pastel paper.
The text is set in Bookman.

Series editor: Tara Walker
Edited by Yvette Ghione
Printed and bound in Singapore

The hardcover edition of this book is smyth sewn casebound.
The paperback edition of this book is limp sewn with a drawn-on cover.

CM 07 0 9 8 7 6 5 4 3 2 1
CM PA 07 0 9 8 7 6 5 4 3 2 1

Library and Archives Canada Cataloguing in Publication

Hood, Susan
    Pup and hound hatch an egg / Susan Hood ; illustrated by Linda
Hendry.

(Kids Can read)
ISBN-13: 978-1-55337-974-4 (bound) ISBN-13: 978-1-55337-975-1 (pbk.)
ISBN-10: 1-55337-974-8 (bound) ISBN-10: 1-55337-975-6 (pbk.)

1. Dogs — Juvenile fiction. I. Hendry, Linda II. Title. III. Series: Kids Can
read (Toronto, Ont.)

PZ7.H758Puh 2007   j813'.54   C2006-902913-X

Kids Can Press is a **lorus**™ Entertainment company

pup and Hound
Hatch an Egg

Written by Susan Hood

Illustrated by Linda Hendry

Kids Can Press

What was that?

"Oink-oink! Moo! Neigh!"

What was the fuss?

4

Oh, look! A birthday!

A new baby filly
stood in the straw —
the wobbliest baby
Pup ever saw!

That spring, more babies
were born each week.
Baby songs rang out:

"Mew!"

"Baa!"

"Peep!"

"Squeak!"

Pup wanted to play.

The mothers said no.

Their babies were little

and needed to grow.

Pup went to the woods
with a hangdog pout.
Hound licked his fur
and kissed his snout.

Pup sat in the grass.

And there by his leg,

he found something round.

Pup found an egg!

Hound knew what to do.

Off to the lake!

Pup rolled the egg gently

so it wouldn't break.

They took it to Duck.

She cried, "Quack! Quack!"

That egg wasn't hers,

so Pup took it back.

Pup pushed the egg
past the pig's pen.
They went up the hill
to old Mother Hen.

But Mother Hen cried,

"Cluck-cluck! Bawk-bawk!"

That egg wasn't hers,

she said with a squawk!

Mother Hen was busy.

She had hatching to do!

She climbed on her nest
and told them to shoo!

Pup rolled the egg

past bales of hay.

Then suddenly,

that egg got away!

Over the hilltop,

over the knoll,

the egg began

to roll and roll!

It rolled down ...

　　　　and down ...

　　　　　　faster and faster!

Oh, no! Watch out!

What a disaster!

The egg hit a bump

and flew high in the air.

Ducks, chicks and donkeys

all stopped to stare.

They'd never seen

an egg fly — not ever!

Birds flew, but eggs?

How strange! How clever!

Down, down it came

past a panicky jay ...

and thump!

It landed right in the hay.

"Woof!" Pup was glad.

And so was Hound!

They hugged their egg.

They snuggled around.

The egg made a noise.

The dogs jumped back.

The shell broke in two

with a crickety-crack!

It didn't quack
and it didn't cluck.
It wasn't a chick.
And it wasn't a duck.

It made no sound.
It sat blinking its eyes.

It was a turtle!

Surprise! Surprise!

Friends wanted to play.

Pup and Hound said no.

Their turtle was little

and needed to grow.

They watched him and worried
as good parents do.

Now where Pup and Hound go,
Turtle goes, too!